The Ladybird Key Words Reading Scheme is based on these commonly used words. Those used most often in the English language are introduced first—with other words of popular appeal to children. All the Key Words list is covered in the early books, and the later titles use further word lists to develop full reading fluency. The total number of different words which will be learned in the complete reading scheme is nearly two thousand. The gradual introduction of these words, frequent repetition and complete 'carry-over' from book to book, will ensure rapid learning.

The full-colour illustrations have been designed to create a desirable attitude towards learning— by making every child *eager* to read each title. Thus this attractive reading scheme embraces not only the latest findings in word frequency, but also the natural interests and activities of happy children.

Each book contains a list of the new words introduced.

W. MURRAY, the author of the Ladybird Key Words Reading Scheme, is an experienced headmaster, author and lecturer on the teaching of reading. He is co-author, with J. McNally, of 'Key Words to Literacy'—a teacher's book published by The Schoolmaster Publishing Co. Ltd.

THE LADYBIRD KEY WORDS READING SCHEME has 12 graded books in each of its three series—'a', 'b' and 'c'. As explained in the handbook *Teaching Reading,* these 36 graded books are all written on a controlled vocabulary, and take the learner from the earliest stages of reading to reading fluency.

The 'a' series gradually introduces and repeats new words. The parallel 'b' series gives the needed further repetition of these words at each stage, but in a different context and with different illustrations.

The 'c' series is also parallel to the 'a' series, and supplies the necessary link with writing and phonic training.

An illustrated booklet—*Notes for using the Ladybird Key Words Reading Scheme* —can be obtained free from the publishers. This booklet fully explains the Key Words principle. It also includes information on the reading books, work books and apparatus available, and such details as the vocabulary loading and reading ages of all books.

BOOK 7c
The Ladybird Key Words Reading Scheme

Easy to sound

by W. MURRAY

with illustrations
by J. H. WINGFIELD

Ladybird Books Ltd Loughborough

ee

We know the word: **see.**

There are two sounds in the word **see.** They are **s** and **ee.**

s-ee make **see.**

We can make the sounds **b** and **ee.** **b-ee** make **bee.**

Now we can read:

1. Here is a bee.

2. The boy sees the bee.

3. He lets the bee go free.

4. He sees the bee go by the tree.

7214 0031 0

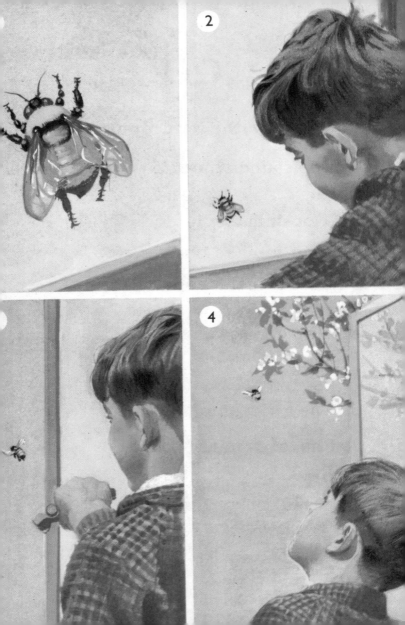

OO

We know the word: **look.**

The sounds **l, oo, k** are in the word **look.**

l-oo-k make **look,**

b-oo-k make **book,**

c-oo-k make **cook.**

Now we can read:

1. Here is a book.

2. The girl wants to cook.

3. She looks in the book.

4. What she sees in the book helps her to cook.

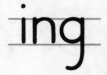

We know the words: **bring, king,** and **going.**

They all end in the sound **ing.**

Now we can read:

1. The king has a ring.

2. The man is fishing.

3. The boy is jumping.

4. The woman is reading.

sh

We know the words: **shop, she, fish** and **wish.**

They all have the sound **sh.**

Now we can read:

1. She looks in the shop.

2. This shop is shut.

3. She has some shells.

4. The fish is in the dish.

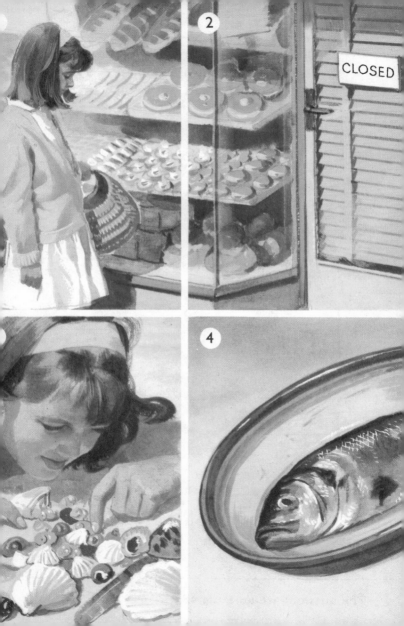

Complete the words as you write
them in your exercise book.   The
pictures will help you.

ee   oo   ing   sh

1 r - - k

2 w - - -

3 bru - -

4 tr - -

5 r - - -

6 h - - k

7 thr - -

8 di - -

The answers are on Page 48.

ea

1. We know the word: **tea.**
   The sounds **t-ea** make the word **tea.**

2. Put the sound **t** after the sound **ea** and you make the word **eat.**

3. We know the word: **sea.**
   The sounds **s-ea** make **sea.**

4. The sounds **s-ea-t** make the word **seat.**

5. The sounds **m-ea-t** make the word **meat.**

6. The sounds **t-ea-p-o-t** make the word **teapot.**

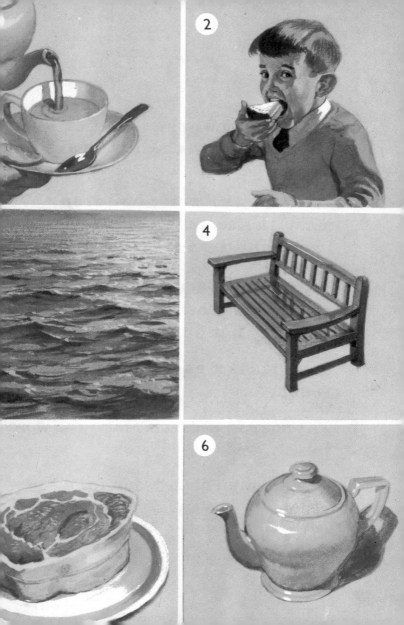

1. We know the word: **chair.** When we start to say **chair** we make the sound **ch.**

2. We know the word: **children.** We make the sound **ch** when we start to say **children.**

3. We know the sounds **ea** and **ch.** **ea-ch** make the word **each.** Each boy has an apple.

4. The sounds **r-ea-ch** make the word **reach.**

5. The sounds **p-ea-ch** make the word **peach.**

6. The children each reach for a peach.

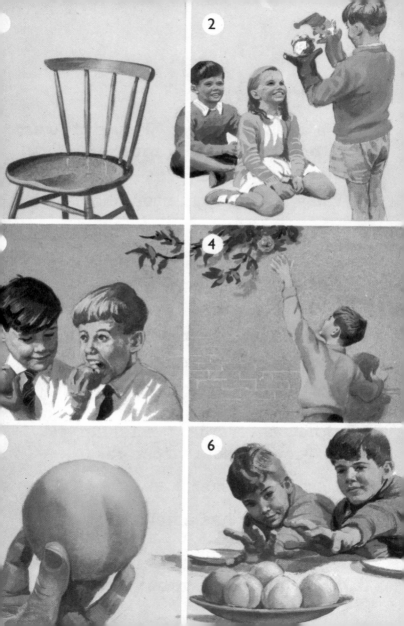

er

We know the words: **Peter, flower, her, brother, sister, mother, father, water.**

They all end in the sound **er.**

1. We can make all the sounds
   t, ea, ch, er.
   The sounds **t-ea-ch-er** make **teacher.**

2. We know the words fish and man.
   Now we can make **fish-er-man.**
   The fisherman is on the pier.

We know the words: farm, help, play and round. Now we can read:

3. Here is a farmer.

4. The farmer has a helper.

5. Here is a player.

6. The children play rounders.

We know the words: **all, ball, call, tell, well, will, hill, doll, pull.**

They all end in the sound **ll.**

Now we can read:

1. The men are by the wall.
   They are all tall.

2. The farmer pulls the bull.

3. The bull pulls the farmer.

4. The teacher gives the boy a bell.

5. The boy rings the bell.

6. He draws a hill and a road.
   Then he draws a mill on the hill.

Complete the words as you write
them in your exercise book. The
pictures will help you.

ea ch er ll

1 b - - ch

2 pat - -

3 we - -

4 l - - f

5 keep - -

6 be - -

7 mat - -

8 numb - -

The answers are on Page 48.

2

4

KEEPER

6

8

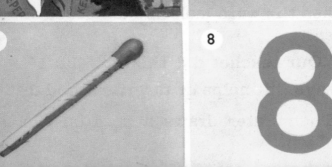

24

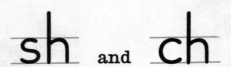

Jane draws a man and two children in a fish and chip shop.

"Look, Peter," she says, "the children are in a fish and chip shop. The man asks the children if they want fish with their chips."

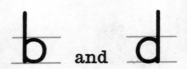

Peter writes the letters **bed**.

"This word is bed," he says. Then he makes the word look like a picture of a bed.

"Our teacher did this at school," he says. "It helps us to write **b** and **d**."

Then Peter draws a man on the bed.

fish and chips

me

so

bed

-e

Peter has the letter **e** on a card.

He says, "I can make **fir** into **fire** with the **e** on this card."

Then he puts the **e** at the end of another word.

"Look," he says, "the **e** at the end makes **pip** into **pipe**. It can make

>　　　**can** into **cane**
>
>　　　**pan** into **pane**
>
>　　　**van** into **vane**
>
>　　　**fir** into **fire**
>
>　　　**tub** into **tube**
>
>　　　and
>
>　　　**pin** into **pine**."

We know the words : **thank, think, three.**

They all start with the sound **th.**

Now we can read :

1. The blue book is thin.

2. This is a thick book.

3. Here is a moth.

4. He has good teeth.

5. It is thick cloth.

6. The number is thirty.

7. The man makes a path.

8. The boy has a bath.

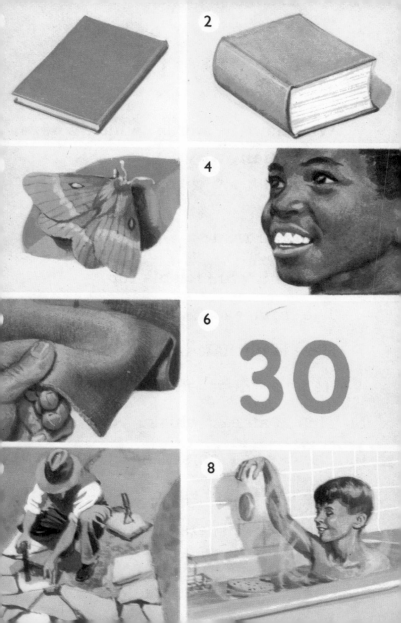

wh

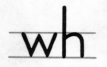

We know the words: **what, where, which, when, why.**

They all start with the sound **wh.**

Now we can read:

1. He has a whip for his top.

2. The farmer looks at his wheat.

3. Here is a whale in the sea.

4. He puts the wheel on the car.

5. This is an egg whisk.

6. The cat has whiskers.

7. The boy has a whistle.

8. The girl whispers to her friend.

Peter and Jane have just had some pictures from their aunt and uncle of their holiday by the sea. There is a letter from Aunty with the pictures. They read the letter in which Aunty tells them that she and Uncle are well. She sends her love to Peter and Jane and their mother and father. Aunty tells them that they may keep the pictures as a present from her. She thinks that the pictures are very good.

"We must write and thank her," says Jane. "Yes, all right," says Peter, "but let us look at the pictures first and then we will write to Aunty and Uncle."

Copy out and complete—

1. The - -ildren have some pictures to l- -k at.
2. - -e has sent them a lett- -.
3. Aunty te- -s them to k- -p the pictures.
4. They are read- - - the letter.
5. They will writ- to - -ank Aunty.

The answers are on Page 48.

The first picture is of the children on the sands, as they go along in a donkey cart. It is an old green cart with big red wheels. Peter and Jane had never been in this donkey cart before.

In the picture the donkey has a hat. On his back he has a red cloth with bells on it. The bells ring as the donkey pulls the cart along. There is a whip in the cart.

"It was a dear little donkey," says Jane. "I do like donkeys." "It did not go very fast," says Peter, "but it was fun."

Copy out and complete—

1. The donkey pu - - s the cart.

2. The wh - - ls are red and the cart is gr - - n.

3. The bells r - - - as the cart is go - - - along.

4. A clo - - is on the donkey's back.

5. There is a - - ip in the cart.

The answers are on Page 49.

Here are some fishing boats going out. The sun is going down as the motor boats put out to sea. Some birds are flying over the fishing boats. The fishermen hope to bring back many fish for the shops. Then there will be fish for anyone to buy and the fishermen will have money.

In the picture, Peter and Jane sit on a wall by the beach with their uncle as they look at the boats. Peter has his kite in his hand

As he looks at the picture, Peter says he would like to go out with the fishing boats one day.

Copy out and complete—

1. They l - - k at the fish - - - boats.
2. Peter and Jane are by the b - - ch.
3. Peter has his kit - in his hand
4. The fish - - men hop - to bring back many fish.
5. There will be fi - - for anyone to buy.

The answers are on Page 49.

This is a picture of the fishermen. Peter and Jane are not in it. The fishermen have come back with many fish in their boats. It is the morning after Peter and Jane saw the fishing boats go out to sea.

The fishermen are working to get the fish out of the boats. They want to get the fish into the shops as soon as they can.

"Would you like to work like that?" Jane asks Peter. "Yes, why not?" says Peter. "I think the men get good pay for their work. They can have a bath and put on other clothes after it."

Copy out and complete—

1. The boats have been out to s--.
2. It is the morn--- after they saw the boats go out.
3. They want to get the fish into the --ops.
4. He thinks the men get g--d money for their work.
5. They can have a ba-- after their work.

The answers are on Page 49.

This is an old mill which Peter and Jane saw when on holiday with their aunt and uncle. A big water wheel works the mill. Aunty and Uncle like to go to the woods, or to this place for a picnic tea when it is very hot.

"We had never been there before," said Jane. "It was nice by the trees. It was not too hot there, but I should not like to go into the water. There would be danger from the mill wheel."

"There were many fish in the water," said Peter. "That man who was fishing had five by the end of the afternoon."

Copy out and complete—

1. It is a picture of an old mi - -.
2. Peter and Jane like a picnic t - -.
3. They had nev - - been there before.
4. In the picture there is a man fish - - -.
5. It is the wheel whi - - works the mill.

The answers are on Page 50.

The children always like playing on the beach. It is best when the sun is out and it is hot. Then the children can take off their clothes to go into the sea or to run and play on the sands.

There are so many things to do. In the picture you can see some donkeys, Punch and Judy, an ice-cream van and the pier. Some children are out in a boat with Jack, and others are looking for shells.

Peter has a jumping game with some other boys. Jane and her friends play with a new, red ball. They all look very happy.

Copy out and complete—

1. They like play - - - on the b - - ch.
2. It is hot - - en the sun is out.
3. Some - - ildren look for - - ells.
4. You can s - - some donkeys.
5. Peter and Jane will put their pictures in a b - - k.

The answers are on Page 50.

When they have seen all the pictures, the children each write to their aunt and uncle to thank them for their letter and the pictures. They tell them how happy they were to be on holiday with them.

Peter writes to his uncle that they are all fit and well and that he and Jane have been to the Zoo. Jane tells Aunty about some new clothes she has had. Then she writes, "Mum and I are going to make some jam. She lets me help her to cook. Dad thinks he would like to keep bees and he has found a book to read about bees. His friend keeps bees."

Copy out and complete—

1. They - - ch write a letter.
2. Jane helps h - - mother to c - - k.
3. They are all fit and we - -.
4. Dad - - inks he would like to keep b - - s.
5. He reads a book - - ich will help him.

The answers are on Page 50.

It is four o'clock. The sun is out again. There has been no rain for days. The two children go out to send off their letters. On their way back they call on a friend. He is going to make a go-cart with some wheels he has found. He tells Peter and Jane that his father will help him to make the go-cart.

"I saw one in a shop," says Peter. "Yes," says his friend, "in some shops they call them Go-Karts. Some Go-Karts have motors in them and others do not."

Copy out and complete—

1. It is not rain - - -.
2. They send off their lett - - s.
3. He has found some - - eels.
4. His father wi - - help him.
5. He saw a Go-Kart in a - - op.

The answers are on Page 51.

Pages 48 to 51 give the answers to
the written exercises in this book.

Page 12

1. rook	2. wing
3. brush	4. tree
5. ring	6. hook
7. three	8. dish

Page 22

1. beach	2. patch
3. well	4. leaf
5. keeper	6. bell
7. match	8. number

Page 32

1. The children have some pictures to
   look at.
2. She has sent them a letter.
3. Aunty tells them to keep the pictures.
4. They are reading the letter.
5. They will write to thank Aunty.

Page 34

1. The donkey pulls the cart.
2. The wheels are red and the cart is green.
3. The bells ring as the cart is going along.
4. A cloth is on the donkey's back.
5. There is a whip in the cart.

Page 36

1. They look at the fishing boats.
2. Peter and Jane are by the beach.
3. Peter has his kite in his hand.
4. The fishermen hope to bring back many fish.
5. There will be fish for anyone to buy.

Page 38

1. The boats have been out to sea.
2. It is the morning after they saw the boats go out.
3. They want to get the fish into the shops.
4. He thinks the men get good money for their work.
5. They can have a bath after their work.

Page 40

1. It is a picture of an old mill.
2. Peter and Jane like a picnic tea.
3. They had never been there before.
4. In the picture there is a man fishing.
5. It is the wheel which works the mill.

Page 42

1. They like playing on the beach.
2. It is hot when the sun is out.
3. Some children look for shells.
4. You can see some donkeys.
5. Peter and Jane will put their pictures in a book.

Page 44

1. They each write a letter.
2. Jane helps her mother to cook.
3. They are all fit and well.
4. Dad thinks he would like to keep bees.
5. He reads a book which will help him.

Page 46

1. It is not raining.
2. They send off their letters.
3. He has found some wheels.
4. His father will help him.
5. He saw a Go-Kart in a shop.

**Revision of sounds
learned in this book.**

ee	oo	ing	sh
ea	ch	er	ll
—e	th	wh	

Now read Book 8a

Words used

This Book 7c provides the link with writing for the words in the Readers 7a and 7b in the Ladybird Key Words Reading Scheme. It also introduces further phonic training.

All the 68 new words in the parallel Readers 7a and 7b are used in this Book 7c, together with others learned in earlier books of the scheme. In addition the following are introduced to assist phonic training:-